BUSTER

by Brent H. Sudduth
Illustrated by Kenneth J. Spengler

To Mom and Dad, for all the love you give me—B.H.S.

To Matthew, my son and fellow bug catcher—K.J.S.

Text copyright © 2003 by Brent H. Sudduth
Illustrations copyright © 2003 by Kenneth J. Spengler
under exclusive license to MONDO Publishing

For information contact:
MONDO Publishing
980 Avenue of the Americas
New York, NY 10018
Visit our web site at http://www.mondopub.com

Printed in the United States of America
03 04 05 06 07 08 09 HC 9 8 7 6 5 4 3 2 1
03 04 05 06 07 08 09 PB 9 8 7 6 5 4 3 2 1

ISBN 1-59034-478-2 (hardcover)   ISBN 1-59034-477-4 (pbk.)

Designed by Edward Miller

Library of Congress Cataloging-in-Publication Data

Sudduth, Brent H., 1964-
Buster / by Brent H. Sudduth ; illustrated by Kenneth J. Spengler.
p. cm
Summary: Buster the firefly is sad that his tail does not light up yet, but when his brothers and sisters are caught by a neighborhood boy, he learns that he has an advantage.
ISBN 1-59034-478-2 (hc. : alk. paper) -- ISBN 1-59034-477-4 (pbk.: alk. paper)
[1. Fireflies--Fiction. 2. Growth--Fiction. 3. Rescues--Fiction.] I. Spengler, Kenneth, ill. II. Title

PZ7.S94342 Bu 2002
[E]--dc21   2002033781

BUSTER

Down the road and behind the big yellow house lived a firefly named Buster.

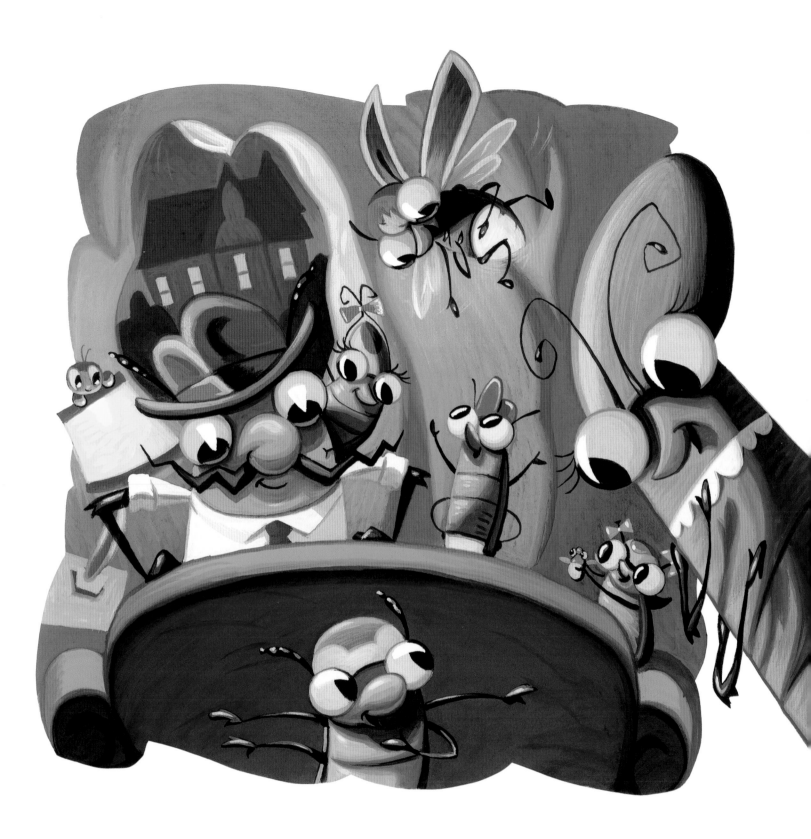

Buster lived in the tree in the backyard with his mother,
his father, and all of his brothers and sisters.

Buster was like most fireflies. He could fly. He had wings. He had a tail. But there was one difference—Buster's tail wouldn't light up.

His mother's tail lit up. His father's tail lit up. All his brothers' and sisters' tails lit up. But Buster could not make his tail light up.

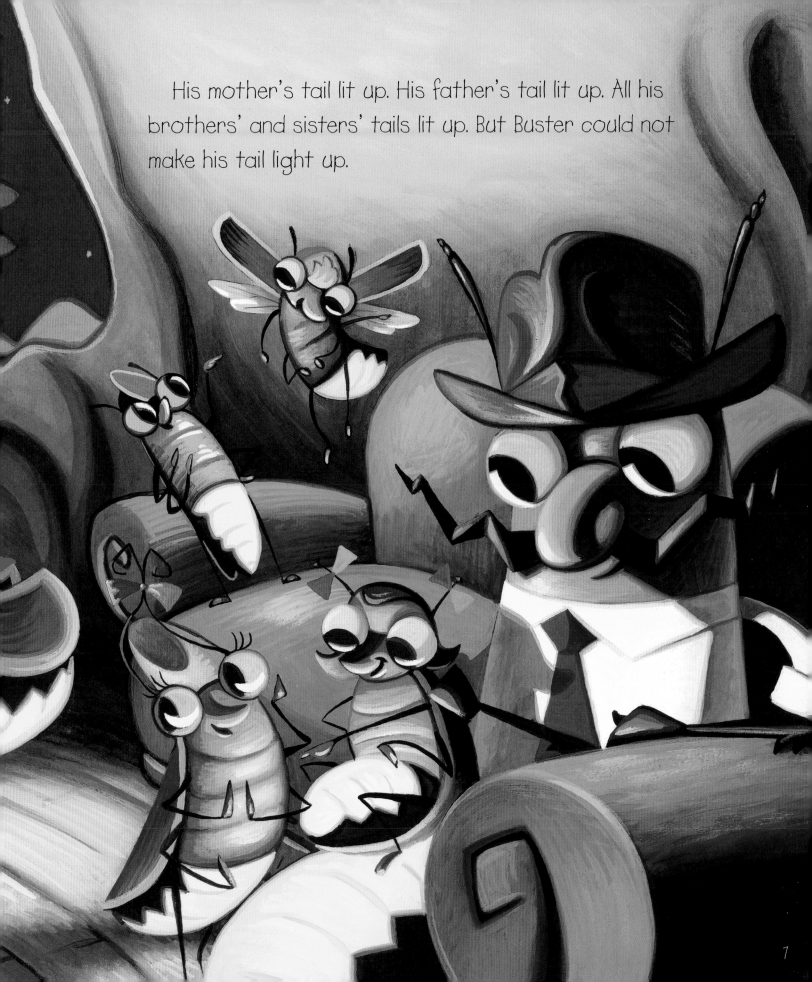

Every day at sunset Buster woke up from his long day's sleep. He was always happy and ready for a deep, dark night.

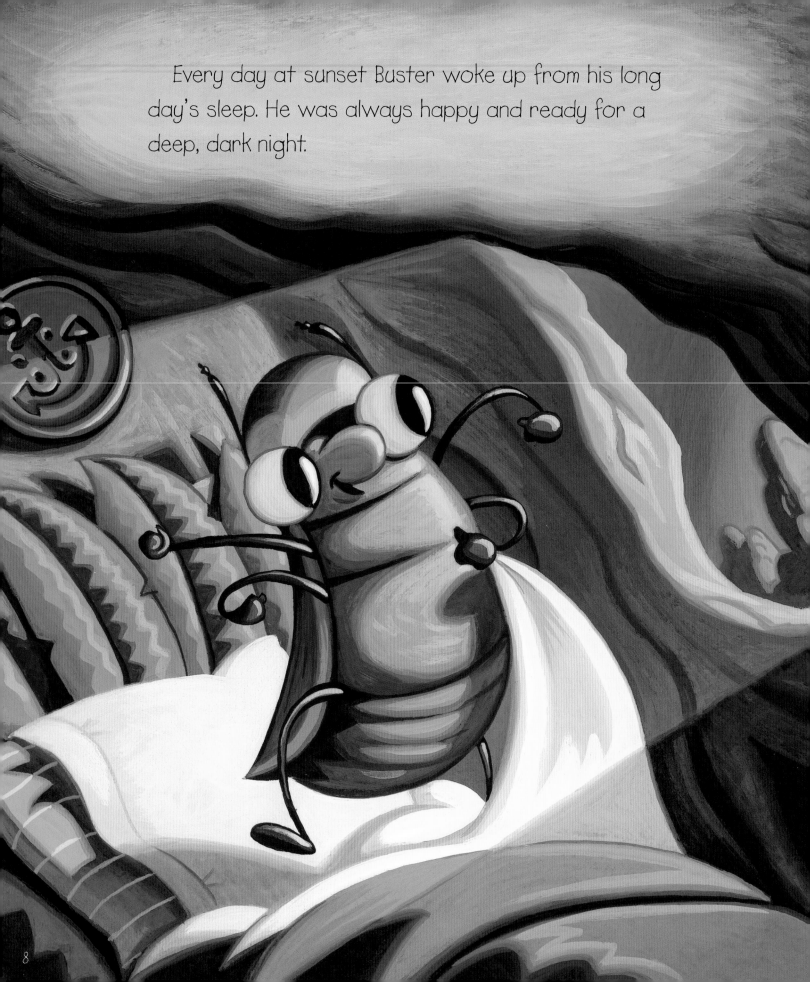

One evening at breakfast, Buster asked his mother,
"When will *my* light come on?"
"Your light will come on when it's time," Mom answered.

"Do I need to eat something to make it come on?" Buster continued.

"You don't need to do anything. Your light will come on by itself. It will come on when your body is ready," Mom explained. "Now go out and play with Willie."

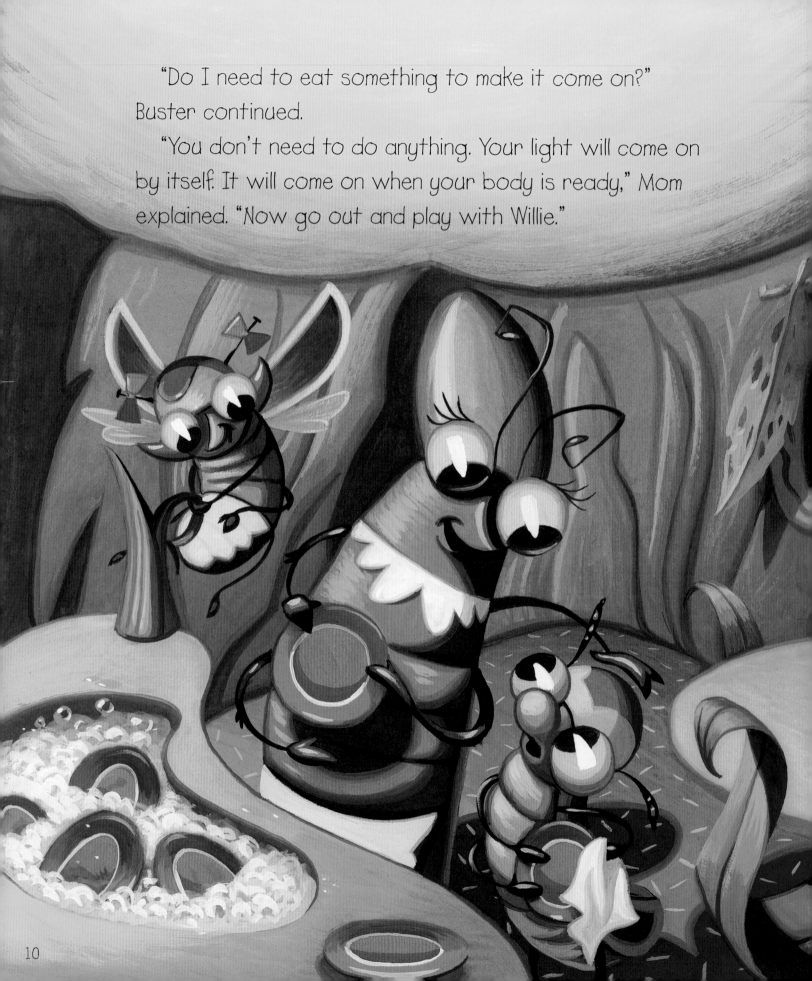

Willie was Buster's best friend. Willie was a gnat.
All night long, Buster and Willie played games like
hide-and-seek and push-the-dandelion.

Willie was great at hide-and-seek!
Some nights it took hours to find him.

12

Buster was good at push-the-dandelion. Some nights he could push over twenty dandelions. But some nights a dandelion would send him flying.

One night Buster and Willie were lying on the grass.
They watched Buster's brothers and sisters play tag.
"My tail is never going to light up," Buster said with
a sad sigh.

"I have an idea," Willie said, picking up a glowworm.
"We can tie him to your tail."
So they did. Or tried to anyway.
"It looks a little silly," Buster whispered.

Just then one of Buster's sisters, Rosie, flew past. She crashed right into a dandelion when she saw Buster. "Hey, look! Buster's light has come on!" Rosie shouted.

Soon the night sky was lit up with Buster's brothers and sisters. Buster turned bright red when his brother Alfie said, "Hey! That's a glowworm tied to his tail!"

Buster sat on the grass feeling sad. Willie sat
down next to him not knowing what to say.

Suddenly they heard screams.
Buster and Willie looked up. Chad, the
boy who lived in the big yellow house,
ran past with a glowing jar full of fireflies!

Willie and Buster followed Chad until he went inside. Then they flew up to his bedroom window.

Chad put Buster's brothers and sisters into a little cage. Buster and Willie sat on the windowsill and watched and waited.

21

Buster and Willie did not know what to do. But then Chad turned his light off and leaped into bed.

Buster climbed over the windowsill
and into the bedroom.

"I have an idea," Buster whispered. "Wait
here for me. If I get caught, go tell my mom."

Buster quietly flapped his wings. He flew
over to the table and hid behind a book.

He sneaked around the book
so he could see the cage. There was
a hook holding the door shut.

Buster flew up to the door and landed on
the hook. When his brothers and sisters saw him,
they flapped their wings excitedly.
"Shhh . . ." Buster warned.

Chad opened his eyes and looked at the cage.
Buster stood perfectly still.

Chad soon fell back to sleep. Buster pushed against
the hook, but it wouldn't budge. He looked over at Willie.
Willie smiled in a way that told Buster he could do it.

So Buster got back under that hook.
He pushed and he pushed and he pushed.
The hook moved just a little—then clank!
The hook fell away.

Buster waved his brothers and sisters out
of the cage. They flew toward the window—just as
Chad woke up! Chad raced over to the window just
in time to see them all fly away . . .

. . . all but Buster and Willie.

Chad grabbed his old butterfly net and slammed it down. Willie and Buster were trapped.

Or were they?

As they flew away, Buster's tail lit up
like a star on the deepest, darkest night.